# FRESH PRINCESS OF BEL AIR

# FRESH PRINCESS OF BEL AIR

TAMEKA HANLEY

Meeks Kreations

Fresh Princess of Bel- Air

# *Dedication Page*

TO EVERYONE WHO FEELS LIKE THEIR VOICE
IS UNHEARD...I HEAR YOU.

AUTHOR TAMEKA HANLEY

# *Acknowledgements*

FIRST AND FOREMOST, I ABSOLUTELY MUST THANK GOD. WITHOUT HIM, I AM NOTHING.

THANK YOU TO MY AMAZING FAMILY FOR BEING MY SUPPORT AND MY BACKBONE.

WHEN YOU ARE DOWN TO NOTHING, GOD IS UP TO SOMETHING. NEVER GIVE UP!

# Table of Contents

DEDICATION
ACKNOWLEDGEMENTS

# *Prologue*

## QUE THE MUSIC

A cool breeze filters through the streets of Bel Air, California causing the tall palm trees to sway. In the close distance, the Hollywood sign towers over plush green mountains. The sky is filled with dreamy burnt orange as the sunset lurks along the horizon. A jet black Chevy Trailblazer coasts up a classy, windmill-like driveway.

The SUV swoops around a massive, renaissance inspired water fountain and comes to a stop in front of a mansion. The castle-like silhouette of the eight bedroom estate is constructed with gorgeous grey stone and massive windows that are layered perfectly in all the right places. A tennis court, pool with connecting hot tub, and basketball court are in clear view. The backseat window of the SUV slowly rolls down, revealing a beautiful six-teen-year-old girl, Alexa Baldwin. She pulls off her black   Ray- Bans and her cherry apple red stained lips crack into a smile. The "Carters' Apesh*t" blares through her ear pods.

*Stack my money fast and go*
*(fast, fast, go)*
*Fast like a Lambo*
*(skrrt, skrrt, skrrt)*
*I be jumpin' off the stage, ho*
*(jumpin', jumpin', hey, hey)*
*Crowd better savor (crowd goin' ape, hey)*

Still smiling, Alexa pops her ear pods out one at a time. She roams over to the water fountain, then the tennis court and the pool, her eyes getting bigger and her smile growing cheesier with every glance.

*No Way* - she all but shouted.

Entranced by what she was seeing, her driver, Henry Staton, who happens to also be her new butler and close friend of the family, exits the SUV. He's giving all the men in black vibes wearing an all-black suit and sunglasses. Just then he pops open Alexa's door and extends his hand out to her.

"Right this way Madame Baldwin," he recites, helping her get out of the vehicle and sounding very much like Harry Potter.

Alexa jumps out. Her feet, adorned by Timberland boots, stomp loud at the ground. She gently adjusts her daisy duke shorts and crop hoodie that reads *#datbih*. While tucking her fly away hairs back into her curly mane she looks up at Henry.

"Just Alexa."

Henry responds with an odd look. Before he can get out another word Alexa smacks on her gum, grabs her fanny pack and begins to make her way to the huge Cherrywood front doors. Already being called a Madame, she had a feeling her life would soon be turned upside down.

# CHAPTER 1

"I STILL FALL ON MY FACE SOMETIMES AND I CAN'T COLOR INSIDE THE LINES 'CAUSE I'M PERFECTLY INCOMPLETE. I'M STILL WORKING ON MY MASTERPIECE."
-JESSIE J

# I Got in One Little Fight and My Dad Got Scared

Alexa Marie Baldwin is my full name. I am 16 years old. I'm practically grown (in my head that is). After losing several debates with my dad about my maturity I've come to terms with the fact that I'm growing up and not quite a grown up yet. Shamelessly, I proved his point with a recent argument, but I'll explain more later.

I hail from Harlem, New York, been there all of my sixteen years of life, until now. I've never been the fighting type of chick but this specific time was different. I reached my boiling point with this hefa named Vanessa Clark. Vanessa and I go all the way back to P.S. 45 Elementary School and quickly became best friends. Vanessa was always the little mualotto girl that had everything. On top of that, she had gorgeous green eyes and golden blonde baby doll hair. Meanwhile, I couldn't even pull my wild curly mane into a ponytail without having to pour a gallon of hair products in first. She had all the best dolls and I had the best dresses.

I would beg my dad to take me to her house every day after school so we could play *America's Next Top Model* with her Barbie's. Not that I didn't have any dolls, I just didn't have nearly as many as she did, and the fact that she handled her dolls carelessly. I couldn't risk her doing Sasha and Theresa wrong as they were my favorite dolls.

Despite how different our economic status was, we brought out the best in each other. She would complement my hair texture and clothes constantly. I would play with her hair and give her the dresses that I no longer wanted so that my Nana could buy me more. I realized at a young age that was the only way to get her to buy new dresses for me.

I never felt like a misfit when Vanessa was around. We were inseparable and our playdates were the best. I thought we were going to be best friends for life. So what happened? Our end of the year kindergarten spelling bee - that's what happened.

My Dad had finally been able to convince my mom to attend one of my school functions. The thought of my mom leaving her room and seeing me kill my spelling bee was my 6-year-old dream. She had already missed my first Halloween Parade, class Christmas party, and the annual Mommy and Me Mother's Day breakfast. You would think I would stop looking into the crowd and continue to be disappointed. Nope. Each time my teacher opened the doors to our classroom, my eyes would dart to the door. I would watch as all the other mommies eagerly embraced their daughters or sons. I'd imagine what that would feel like. It was like my teacher already knew my mom wouldn't show up so she'd automatically send my dad the information. Still, I kept that glimmer of hope. My dad would stroll in with a huge smile on his face and scoop me into his arms. He'd wipe the tears that escaped my eyes and in an instant all was right within the world.

When he told me my mom had said she was coming to my spelling bee, he seemed to be more excited than I was. At this point my mom hadn't showed up for any of my school events, so my six year old self became a bit reluctant to share in the excitement. But despite the disappointments all I wanted was to make my mommy proud. Vanessa and I were besties, so I told her everything. We both squealed with excitement when I told her she would finally meet my mom. The spelling bee was a few days away and I was filled with anticipation.

My dad taught me that the key to spelling was memorization. So out came the index cards, and primary colored markers. He was right by my side as I wrote each word down. I color coordinated them from the easiest to the hardest words. He was my coach and he would even quiz me as I jumped rope. For some reason that was the only way the words stuck with me. We worked hard the entire duration of our study sessions. During my playdates with Vanessa, my dad would create games using the words for us to play. The closer the big day of the bee came the more confident I became. I was going to win that spelling bee and make my momma proud.

On the day of the spelling bee my mom had finally came out from her room. She revived my tangled curls and brushed them into a sleek ponytail adding a lavender bow that was drenched in rhinestones. When she was finished with my hair, she picked out my lavender princess dress and clear gel sandals. A radiant smile beamed from her face. For a short moment in time I had a mom. During the bee I would pinch myself to make sure I wasn't dreaming this all up. My mom was really there sitting, perched in the row with the rest of the proud parents yelling their baby's name whenever they spelled their word right. I was killing the competition while everyone was dropping out like flies. It was down to Vanessa and me. We had promised each other that no matter what we'd be happy for whoever wins.

"Alexa, your last word is Exclaimed."

"Exclaimed," I shakily repeated back.

My confidence immediately flew off in the distance. I had studied every word but that one. How could my teacher Ms. Honey forget to put it on the list? I looked over at my dad. Both him and I knew the word list by heart and could recite it front ways and back ways. I thought that maybe it was on the list and we missed it. I had no time to try and play detective as I had to spell the word. My dad gave me a look that said - *regardless of the outcome he was very proud*.

I panned my eyes over to my mom. She mouthed you got this baby. I gulped. This was it and I knew I had to give it my best shot. Besides, if I didn't know it, I knew for sure Vanessa didn't either. There was still going to be a chance for me to win. It would have to come to a tie breaker.

"Ex-cl-am-d, exclaimed?"

"I'm sorry sweetie, but that's not correct," Ms. Honey sadly replied.

My head instantly dropped. I peaked over at my dad again. He motioned for me to pick my head up. I inhaled deeply as I slowly allowed my head to return back to its natural position. I inwardly chanted *I can still win this; it's not over,* in my head just about a million times. Vanessa was up. She nervously looked around before hearing…

"Vanessa, your word is exclaimed."

No one seemed to notice her nervous glance around the room. Her eyes landed on her mother. She cleared her throat, not losing her eye contact.

"Exclaimed," She paused momentarily.

"Ex-cl"

I stared at her and then my eyes met up with the target of her attention. Her mother began to mouth the rest of the letters.

" – ai-med, Exclaimed."

"That's correct!"

Ms. Honey beamed from head to toe as cheers and applause roared from the small audience filled with parents.

My jaw dropped. I couldn't believe that backstabbing wench would steal my chance to shine. Vanessa's mom ran up and bear hugged her, making dramatic sobbing noises identical to the ungodly sounds of Loretta Divine in all her movies.

My mom was silent the entire car ride home. I already knew what was about to happen. Back to solitary confinement she would go. And she did just that when we got back home. I ran to my room and cried. Even though

Vanessa blatantly cheated, I still couldn't shake the cold disappointed look she gave me the moment Vanessa was declared the winner.

From then on Vanessa was appointed my enemy. I laughed at her sorry attempts to get me to talk to her. She was dead to me then and she's dead to me now.

Anyway, back to this stupid fight. First of all y'all, there's very little that anyone can say or do to me that would seriously get my blood boiling. Calling me stank, boogie, fake, or a thot has little effect on me. *Sticks and stones may break my bones but words will never hurt me* is what I said to myself every time the Queen of Rumors had a hard time keeping my name out of her mouth. Not many people knew what rattled me. And thanks to my resting bitch face not many people were brave enough to try.

Unfortunately, we shared secrets at some point during our short lived friendship so Vanessa knew exactly what to say to catch my attention. This Siddity Barbie wannabe told everyone in my sophomore class that my mama was a bum that wanted nothing to do with me.

*Oh she wanna talk about mama, its mother time, okay*, I said to myself. She knew anything related to my mama was and still is a very sensitive subject matter. Hearing the snickers of some and seeing the pity filled glances of others when I walked down the hall had me seeing red. I snatched my gold bamboo earrings out of my ears, shoved them in the back pocket of my Levi's and speed walked to her locker. Sensing that someone was behind her, she shoved the remainder of the textbooks that were in her arms into her locker and slammed it shut. She folded her arms after she turned around with a smirk on her face. With no words...BAM! I decked her right in her pretty green eye. She instantly slammed backwards onto the lockers.

It was so unexpected, and I honestly didn't mean to hit her. My plan was to just talk to her and tell her to quite running her mouth about me but when I saw her, it was like all the past memories of her constantly trying to pull me down instantly came to my mind. I recalled her purposely running against me for Miss Sophomore, or for captain of the cheerleading squad, trying to steal my boyfriend, hell even my friends. It wasn't as if I wasn't going through enough with family shenanigans at home. Her envy and pettiness contributed to my already messy life. And look, enough is enough. I was over it so yes, I hit her. I punched her and I'm proud.

Y'all should've seen her face when she realized what happened. Ha! She looked at me with shock and anger as she held her eye. Before she could retaliate, my Spanish teacher Ms. Garcia yanked us both up and dragged us to the principal's office. Let's just say there's now a large ring of blue and purple to accessorize one of those green eyes she likes to flaunt.

I know what you're thinking. I'm impulsive. I shouldn't have let her get to me. What happened to sticks and stones Alexa? Well screw you. Y'all know if anyone was to say anything malice about your mother, you would go ham, too. I don't care how old you are, or how close you are to her, don't nobody talk about my mama.

So now here I am. In frickin' Bel Air, California.
I mercilessly begged, telling my father I would change my ways but he shouted. My ears are still ringing.

"You're moving with your Uncle and Aunty in Bel Air Alexa and that's the end of it!"

I may live in a mansion and have a British butler but I will always be me - Witty, goofy, blunt Alexa Marie Baldwin from Westford Harlem.  Unapologetically

# CHAPTER 2

"Forgive me, forgive me, I've been going too hard in your city
So forgive me, 'cause I'm not teary.
-Chloe&Halle

# In Westford Harlem Born and Raised

Don't get me wrong - Bel Air is gorgeous and I'm definitely putting this mansion on the Gram but Harlem is my home. I don't belong here with these snooty Barbie and Kens. I can still hear my Dad say...

"Lex, don't worry about what anyone else says about you. Only you can determine your worth, be confident in that."

Why couldn't I have just listened to him? How did I fall so far from the girl I used to be? The girl that glided down the halls of Saints High School beaming as I pranced along, holding onto the arm of Roger McClain, aka the love of my life, but I'll gush more about him later. I was the girl who dreamed of going to Juilliard so that I could become the next Misty Copland. That Girl?

Okay, so enough with the violins. Let's take it back where it truly all began for me, Saints High, sophomore year. I had just turned sixteen, had my besties Serenity, Laila, and Kyrie *#mybestfriendsarebetterthanyours* but most importantly I had Roger the junior varsity star of Saints High Football Team, and honey, you couldn't tell me shid.

"5, 6, 7, 8, and a 1 and 2 roll 3, 4, sway 5, 6, 7, 8," I belted out charismatically as I watched my squad with hawk eyes, pacing around each member.

"Good Chelsea. Watch your timing, Kiara. It's like a two second pause before that roll."

"Again, from the top, 5, 6 7, 8, let's go!"

Varying colors and textures of long hair swung left to right. Precise hip rolling mirrored with graceful, yet sharp arms, floated in rhythmic directions. Hands were gliding smoothly across each of my dancer's chests and bodies. Each hand accentuated their voluptuous curves and legs. Whoever said young girls don't develop their bodies until later *lied* okay, cause' we had all the booty.

My eight counts abruptly stopped. I yelled, letting out a frustrated sigh.

"Stop! Y'all look dead. I mean c'mon give me life. Y'all lookin' like y'all tired. Y'all tired?"

They whined in unison.

"No Captain Lex."

"So let's cut the laziness and get to work. Full Out. From the top."

I counted them in. Again the girls prodded their bodies poetically with each move. But this time the attitude and the effort were there. We truly had so much damn swag.

"Yaasss y'all! That's what I'm talkin' bout."

I ran over to my phone that was plugged in to my Samsung block speaker.

"Hey Siri, play Drop Top In the Rain by Ty Dolla $ign."

The seductive yet upbeat song began to play. Leading my team I rolled my hips, slow and sharp, drowning all of me in each move.

*Droptop in the rain, woah, woah*
*Droptop in the rain, woah,*
*woah*
*Droptop in the rain, oh yeah,*
*yeah, yeah.*

They followed my lead repeating exactly what I did. Each hair swayed, body roll and hand movement was perfectly echoed. We went hard all the way through the song.

"And that's a wrap. Good Job ladies."

Smiles and distinct chatter broke out amongst us. High fives went around to each of the girls as sweat glistened off of our faces and foreheads with weaves sweating out.

As the captain of the vivacious Prancing Dolls Majorette Dance Team, the youngest captain thus far might I add, I made it my daily mission to push my team to our absolute wits end. But I still gave them love and encouragement in times when we desperately needed it. Now don't get me wrong, everything wasn't always rainbows and sprinkles between us. Nevertheless, that was my squad and we always had each other's backs on the floor. **SQUAD**

Whenever I danced, all was well in my world. I forget about everything and completely lose myself in the music. I commanded my body to surrender to each move with ease, precision and swag. Majorette dancing was just the tip of the dance ice burg for me. It's what connected me to two of my best friends Serenity and Laila. We coincidently auditioned together our freshman year. I was number 4, Ren was number 7 and Lay was number 9. We just so happened to be put in a group together when the time came to audition.

We fed off each other like magnets. You could feel the electricity in the room as we performed the routine. The judges were completely captivated by our routine as if they hadn't seen it done a million times. They had, but not like how we performed the routine. Our audition time seemed to have come and gone. Before we knew it, we were huddled together waiting to see who all made the team. We barely knew each other yet we had already felt like sisters. It literally felt like a celebration every time we linked up.

Even though the numbers of the girls who made the team hadn't been posted in the hall outside of the Braxton Sylver Auditorium yet, we were already feeling like we had it in the bag. And we did.

One of the judges finally came out holding the paper with the results in her hand and everyone swarmed around her like bees. One after one, girls took their turns, seeing if their number was on there. You could tell who made it and who didn't based off of each girl's expression after glancing at the numbers on the paper. You would've thought it was the Holy Grail.

It was our turn to see the results. We held each other's hands and slowly strolled to it. TAHDOW! Our numbers were the first three on there! We squealed.

Yup, those are my girls, and they will never be replaced by some Barbie wannabe.

My boy Kyrie fell right in shortly after our auditions. We were lab partners for Mr. DeAblo's physical science class. He was dumb funny. Mr. DeAblo would spend most of the class time yelling at us for geekin' instead of focusing on the lab he just assigned.

Kyrie would instantly take the blame and two minutes later we'd be acting up again.

"My fault, Mr. DeAblo."

Kyrie and I instantly connected from the jump. It was more of a friend connection for me. He, on the other hand, wanted to get with me, which landed him further in the friend zone. Don't get me wrong - Kyrie was stupid swaggy but I already had eyes on Aaron. Besides, he and Ren made a dope couple. If you ask me, Kyrie was just that dude, The Homie.

It's because of Kyrie that I finally spoke to Aaron. I actually spoke to him. Up until then, Aaron and I would just say a friendly "wassup" wheneva we past each other in the hallway. Kyrie pushed me to work my finesse and spit my game.

"What game, Kyrie? Helloo it's me we're speakin' of, not you."

"Lex, why you doubtin' yourself? Look at you. You one of the baddest freshmen at this school."

Just then his gaze went directly to my butt as I smacked him on his arm.

"Boy!"

"Ow," he said, rubbing his now bruised arm.

"Dang! A brotha can't give you a compliment?"
Rolling my eyes I responded.

"Mmhmm. Thanks, Ky."

"I'm serious Lex, he's a cool dude. I mean if you want me to I'll put the word in."

"Please don't."

I grabbed my American Literature textbook, a few more pencils, and notebook from out of my locker.
"He's coming to your birthday party tonight. I'll talk to him then, aight?"

The bell rang, vibrating loudly through all the halls.

"Let me go before Ms. Kuffman says something about me being late again. I'll catch you later, birthday boy."

I kissed his cheek and we did our special handshake. Slap, slap, kriss kross slap, salute.

Ky's party was lit. It was a classic house party at a bomb house, his house, which was close to a mansion, something he still doesn't like to admit. Why? It beats me. Anyway, yes this party. Super bomb, all decked out in beautiful décor to display the *Coming to America* theme.

Kyrie always considered himself to be some type of Don. His parents did, too, so they always made sure he got what he wanted. He was indeed Prince Kyrie.

Just about everyone at school was there, including Aaron. He was looking so fine in his custom African attire. I noticed the very moment he stepped foot in the door. Ren, Laila, and I had been the first ones there of course. We made it a point to show up a few hours early to help set up and hype my boy up. It was his day and we wanted him to truly soak up the moment.

"Ayeeee."

The DJ was playing all the hits and everyone was gettin' it on the marble dancefloor. Kyrie was in the middle of the floor. All the girls was competin' for his attention. From splits to twerking headstands, I mean, they were playing no games. The three of us smiled and shook our heads as we watched Ky eat up all the attention. And he wasn't the only one getting some play. Guys had been pretty much beggin' for one of us to dance with them. One by one they would come and whisper in one of our ears.

"You tryna dance?"

Ren was always the first one to break the ice and dance with someone. For me, it was all about the song. If my song was playing I would maybe consider it. Most of the time I'd like to just whine my waist in my little corner by myself or two step with Ky, which would just cause more guys to ask me to dance.

Me and Ky had just finished vibin' to a song and I was just about to take a break when the DJ smoothly transitioned to another hit.

 *Oops I done fell so deep 'cause*
*Everyone falls in love sometimes*
*I don't know 'bout you but it ain't*
*a crime*

Ky instantly started grinning. He knew that was my song. You know that one song that always seems to get you in the dancing mood? Yup, that was it. As if my hips had a mind of its own, I began to whine, effortlessly hittin' each bom, bom, bom, bom.

Ky shouted, hyping me up.

"Get it Lex!"

Before I knew it I felt someone behind me, pulling me closer to them. I frowned, quickly glancing to see who had the audacity to run up behind me before asking. My heart fluttered, when I saw that it was Aaron. Thankfully he hadn't noticed my initial hesitation. Wanting it to stay that way, I smoothly rolled into an arch and worked my hips like my life depended on it.

Needless to say he was hooked from that moment on. Not to mention we had a ton in common. But what I liked most about him was that he wasn't just some athlete who wanted to run game. He was a legit scholar in all AP classes and treated me like the princess that I am. Besides Ky, he was and still is the only boy that my dad has approved of. I may have been exiled to Bel Air but it hasn't stopped Aaron from wanting to be with me. We both agreed to test out a long distance relationship so that's what we're doing. Yes I'm going to miss him and vice versa but with frequent Facetime and texting we should be straight. Surprisingly, my dad promised me that once I "get my act together" he'll personally fly all my crew and my boo out to Bel Air.

I can't believe I have to start all over. Finding friends was hard enough, now I have to attempt to make friends again. It is times like this I wish I had a mom so she could tell me that everything will be fine, that my friends and boyfriend will not change, that I will not change and that despite it all, she's still proud of me.

There is a part of me that still wants to be connected to my mom. That is until I recall my birthdays, Christmases past, and recitals with her locked in her bedroom as my Dad tried so hard to keep a smile on his face for me. I never knew why my mom wanted nothing to do with me or why she chose drugs over her family. My dad fought so long for her, bending over backwards to pay for her continual rehab along with everything else. He spent long work hours at both of his jobs, which allowed me to spend very little time with him. During those times I would pop in the Center Stage DVD and watch it on repeat. I memorized the final performance scene, the infamous dance that incorporated Michael Jackson's The Way You Make Me Feel. I loved every bit of it. It was as if that moment had awakened something in me that I never knew was inside of me. I knew then that I wanted to become a dancer.

My dad bought me a blush pink standup mirror for my sixth birthday as he thought it would inspire me to start styling my own hair. He was done putting pigtails in my hair every day and believe me, so was I. The beautiful mirror had no effect on my drive to do my hair. Instead, I would find myself twirling, then plie'ing, leaping in front of the mirror. On the weekends I'd do almost everything while standing on my toes.

Family ties were extremely loose on my Dad's side and you can forget about my mom's side. They despised the fact that my mother was even trying be a mother so I didn't exist to them. It wasn't that they didn't know about me. My father and my mother were high school sweethearts that tied the knot right after they crossed the stage and everything was peaches and cream. The pregnancy was a slip up but they were convinced that they would still make things work.

My mom, Anastasia Lex Baldwin, was a registered nurse and my dad worked as an assistant to an Executive Manager at Columbous Records, a major label company. His family was haters and they looked and talked down on him because he was an assistant. They felt like that wasn't a man's job and that a man shouldn't have to answer to anyone. They were extremely old school. Everyone, that is, except my Uncle Bradley. He was supportive of my father and little did the family know that within one year my dad would be promoted to Executive, which made him the first BLACK man to head the label.

That's my daddy. It was us against the world. Our relationship has definitely been tested over the years but I greatly admire him. I know that whenever I need him, in a blink of an eye, he'd be there for me. As much as I hate that I'm forced to now start over in Bel Air, I know he just wants the best for me.

I guess I need to accept the fact that I'm in Bel Air now. Let's see how the wannabe Brady Bunch likes me now.

*Y'all ready?*

# CHAPTER 3

"WHATEVER IT IS, IT FEELS LIKE IT'S LAUGHING AT ME THROUGH THE GLASS OF A TWO-SIDED MIRROR. WHATEVER IT IS, IT"S JUST LAUGHING AT ME AND I JUST WANNA SCREAM."

-RIHANNA

# I Looked At My Kingdom - I was Finally There

BRADLEY WHITE casually pulls up his tailored pant legs and plops his feet on a footrest. His wife BETHANY WHITE sashays into the industrial size living room equipped with state of the art décor and furniture. A pure white grand piano sits smack dab in the middle of the room as she hands him a glass of finely-aged red wine. She teases him with a smile, showing off her perfectly straight white teeth.

"To another job well done."

He responds as they clink glasses.

"And I couldn't have done it without you."

"Damn right."

He chuckles and swoops her into his arms. They share a passionate kiss for a heated amount of time.

"Umm-hmph, Madame Baldwin sir," Henry announces.

The couple instantly breaks away from their kiss. Adjusting his shirt, Bradley hastily replies.

"Please see her in Henry."

Within moments, Henry returns with Alexa following behind him. She scans the room with her cellphone, changing the phone mode to SELFIE, flashing duck lips and taking several wannabe diva pictures. Both Bradley and Bethany stand up.

"Yes Honey. I have arrived."

"See this is the problem with you millennials. Always have to do it for the Instachat."

Bradley grips her up in a bear hug.

"Uncle Brad, Promise not to say Instachat eva again okay."

"Yeah, when you stop getting into trouble young lady."

Alexa wiggled herself out of her Uncle's arms and put her hands on her hips.

"Look...y'all can relax with all that young lady, madam stuff. Just-"

"Manners. In this house we use them."

Bethany quickly chimed in, cutting Alexa off.

"Well hello to you, Aunt Beth."

Alexa murmured something sarcastic back under her breath.

"Excuse me?"

Bethany folded her arms as if it were a natural instinct, while Alexa immediately reminded herself of *Operation get the homies flown to Bel Air*. She plastered a smile on her face and hugged her Aunt but Bethany doesn't budge and her arms remain folded. After the two second embrace Alexa quickly backed away.

"Auntie you look gorgeous darling."

Bethany snickers before extending a short smile as Bradley beams and chimes in.

"Look at you. My baby niece all grown up."

He does a 360 scan. Alexa does several model poses, graciously taking in the attention. Bethany can't hold back.

"Almost grown. Let's not get too carried away Bradley."

Restraining herself from rolling her eyes, Alexa reads a text that just came through on her phone.

"You're right, Aunt Beth, cause best believe when I am grown, I'mma have me a dope ass..."

Bradley sees Bethany's face frown up from the corner of his eye. He quickly cuts in before his wife unleashes hell on his niece.

"Wait until you see your cousin Caroline. Henry show Alexa her room please."

He chuckles to clear the awkward tension in the room. Henry gives her his *I Dream of Genie* nod and gathers a few pieces of Alexa's oversized luggage.

"Right this way Madame Baldwin."

"My room? Oh I'm goin' LIVE," she replied, bursting with excitement, barely able to unlock her phone.

Alexa's aunt and uncle were both in their forties. They never told her their exact ages but according to Aunt Bethany, she's only 30 and Uncle Bradley is "old enough."

Uncle Bradley and my dad have always been tight. While everyone else in my dad's family stuck their noses up at us, Uncle Bradley showered us with nothing but love and support. He's the only one in the family that truly had money, everyone else was just flexin'.

Bethany and Bradley were also business partners, owning an elite law firm, one of the best law firms in the State of California. He used to fly me out to Cali every other summer, until he met and married my Aunt Bethany. She hated me from the first time she laid eyes on me. I was the ghetto niece that her husband adored.

When my dad and Uncle were discussing my exile, I overheard her on the phone pleading for them to reconsider the decision. My Uncle, as always, had my dad's back, and well, here I am at his mansion. Like I said before, I won't be anyone but me, and I'll never change nor apologize for that - especially to my Aunt Bethany.

Bethany paced back and forth with her hands glued to her hips, shaking her head.

"LIVE? The nerve of her to prance in here like-"

Bradley loudly exhaled as he already knew he was in for it. The subject of his niece usually ignited a hostile fire within his wife.

"Honey, please don't start."

"That language and her shirt?" Bethany continued with disgust.

"Hoodie."

"Whatever the hell it was."

Bethany rebuttals back and stops pacing long enough to fan herself. Bradley pulls her into his arms, and caresses her cheek. Her angry eyes immediately soften as she stares back at his as he gently asks for a small favor.

"Just give her a chance. Please."

She gives in to his comfort and responds with a kiss.

"Okay," she whispers just before she exhales, grabs her glass of delicious wine and downs it.

The butler, Henry, is giving Alexa the grand tour, sounding slightly annoyed as he has probably given this tour a million times.

"And to your right, Madam, you will find another bathroom."

"Look Hen, we talked about this. I get it. You're forced to be proper. But please just call me Alexa. And don't worry about the rest of the tour I got it from here."

"As you wish, Alexa, I'll see to bringing your luggage to your room."

"Thanks."

She jokingly curtsied before Henry scurried away with her suitcases. Chuckling to herself, she walked over to a wall covered with classic black and white photos of her Uncle with his upscale colleagues at several events. Her eyes landed on a photo of her Uncle with Michelle Obama. In the photo, he was smiling, standing beside her at her launch party for her memoir, _Becoming_.

Just then her cousin, Caroline enters the room.

"Oh my God Alexa! You're here!"

Caroline kisses Alexa on each cheek. Alexa instantly wipes them away.

"In the flesh."

Alexa was curt with her response, turning her attention back to the photos while Caroline looked her over, truly intrigued by what she saw.

"My what an outfit. I love it. You Harlem girls have so much spunk."

Alexa's eyes snap in Caroline's direction. She stares at Caroline who is giddy with excitement.

"Gee thanks?"

Restraining herself from slapping her ignorant cousin, she resumes looking at the framed photos on the wall.

"Michelle Obama personally mailed that one to us. Licked the stamp and all."

Seeing that her cousin wasn't going to let up, she mustered up all of the sarcasm she had left.

"Oh my God. No way."

"Yes Sister. The girls were so jelly. Speaking of, they are just dying to meet you. It's going to be great. We'll all hang out. Oh, and I'll get you on the cheer team."

Caroline is beyond fueled up with excitement but Alexa wasn't having it.

"Yeah, no."

"Don't worry. We'll teach you all of the techniques."

"Right. Listen, I would love to hear more about Holly, Becky, and Ann but I'm just tryna go see my room so...text me?"

Acting as if something important on her phone popped up, Alexa looks down at it.

"Sure. And they're names are..."

Alexa dashes down the hall, popping her gum along the way when Caroline pulls her phone from out of her back pocket of her jeans.

"Wait! I don't have your..."

She stops midsentence, realizing that she's alone.

<<<<<<<<<<<<<<<<<<<<<<<<<<<<<<<<<<<

Caroline, Caroline, Caroline. Where do I even start with her? First off, we don't get along, we never did. She's much like my arch enemy Vanessa except I have to actually tolerate her because she's family. And I use that term loosely. Caroline and I are cousins, same age and all. Very much like her mother, she never liked me since day one. You see, my Aunt Bethany had two kids from a previous marriage, Bryston and Caroline. My Uncle always treated them like they were his. I was so excited that I had a cousin the same age as me. I just knew we were gonna be best cousins but I soon realized that Caroline wanted to change me. She would make me dress like her when we played dress up, or made me play with only her dolls because only her dolls were worthy enough for her to play with.

I asked my dad to stop sending me to my Uncle's house every other summer after I overheard her ask my aunt why she had to play with her ghetto cousin. I was so hurt. I never understood why they were so quick to judge me. But shoot, that's none of my concern anymore. And she can miss me with that wannabe-besties-now-act. #chucksdueces

<<<<<<<<<<<<<<<<<<<<<<<<<<<<<<<<<<<

Alexa's jaw dropped as soon as she stepped into her room. It's literally the room that every teenage girl dreams of. A California King bed filled with a sea of mint green and gold plush pillows. The pillows are matched with a huge shaggy area rug that swallowed up the marble flooring. A white canopy elegantly draped the perimeters of the bed, from top to bottom. The walls were mint green with gold edges. An immaculate bejeweled lamp towered over a Cleopatra-inspired sofa chair topped with fluffy square pillows. A 60-inch flat screen smart TV is mounted on the wall, above one of the six shiny glass-like dressers. In addition to sterling silver electronics, in one corner of the room was a huge vanity equipped with every MAC cosmetic item you can think of and in another corner, a throne chair that was white with gold trimmings.

Alexa flopped face first onto the bed.

She whispered to herself.

"We sure not in Harlem no more Dorothy."

# CHAPTER 4

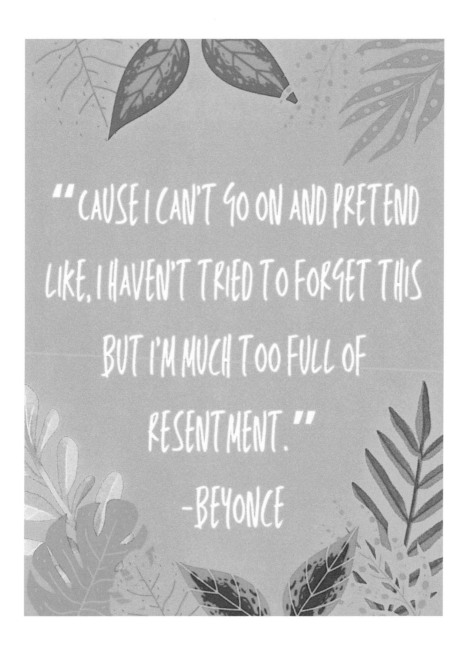

"'CAUSE I CAN'T GO ON AND PRETEND LIKE, I HAVEN'T TRIED TO FORGET THIS BUT I'M MUCH TOO FULL OF RESENTMENT.'"

-BEYONCE

# To Sit at My Throne as the Princess of Bel Air

So y'all got a glimpse of my cousin Caroline, now meet the rest of the fake Brady Bunch clan. Before Caroline, there's my cousin, Bryston. Bryston Reginold White is the boogiest of them all, but I make sure we stay cool so I could get him to get me some sneaks. He takes the definition of sneaker head to a whole notha level. I'm talking every pair of Jordan's there is, Kobe's in every color, Huaraches, Kyrie's, you name it, and he has them. I will never forget the day he brought me my first pair of J's. It was on the very first Christmas I spent with them. He had overheard me asking my dad for them while we were at the mall Christmas shopping. After having to fly us out there, my dad was already on a tight budget.

"Maybe another time pumpkin, I promise."

The sadness in his eyes made the disappointment that much greater. Bryston must have seen it, too, because when it came time to open up gifts, he handed me a beautifully wrapped box. That was the first time I cried happy tears. We had been cool ever since.

Granted, Bryston may have all the flyest gear out there, but he lacks the swag and brains to go with it. No shade or nothin'.

Every time I clowned with him on how lame yet clean he was he his tragic response was the same.

"What Lex? You're tripping. I gets the hunnies."

I would bust out laughin' every time. Poor thing. One time he tried so hard to impress a girl that he baked her a dozen cupcakes shaped like roses. The outside looked bomb but the inside tasted like straight trash. Mainly because he used baking soda instead of baking powder every baking recipe calls for. Like I said, not the brightest crayon in the box.

Destiny White is the newest addition. This 12-year-old is genuinely the dopest of them all, the only one actually. She would always look at me like I was the best cousin in the world. I'd make her giggle an adorable giggle when I made silly faces. I doubt she remembers any of it being that she was only 3 at the time and only 4 when I stopped visiting for the summers. This would honestly be like her meeting me for the first time. Nevertheless, I'll always have a sweet spot for her.

<<<<<<<<<<<<<<<<<<<<<<<<<<<<<<<<<

BRYSTON WHITE, a well-built handsome young man, wearing a retro 90's Nike track suit, comes in whistling as he lugs two massive orange shopping bags that have the Nike logo on them.

Behind him, DESTINY WHITE drags her petite limbs in with a tower of sneaker boxes in her arms, poking her head around them to see where to safely walk. He makes his way to the living room and flops down onto the sofa.

"Whew man. I'm exhausted," he says, stretching his long body across the cushions.

He and Destiny had been at the mall most of the day. After running into the wall for the second time, Destiny slams the boxes down in Bryston's lap.

Just then Bradley and Bethany enter the living room, acknowledging the bags and boxes.

"I can see why."

Destiny runs into his arms.

"It was the longest five hours of my life," she whined.

He looked down at her puppy dog eyes and let out a husky chuckle. Bryston quickly jumped in as he knew his parents would easily fall into his sisters *woe is me* trap and make him out to be the bad guy. He rolled his eyes and expressed his opinion on the matter.

"Now you're just being dramatic."

Destiny narrowed her eyes at him. He had purposely made her his personal slave over the past few hours at the mall and he would pay for it.

"Dramatic? Okay, show them my shoes then," she replied trying her hardest to hide her smirk.

She threw the baited hook and was about to catch a big fish. The reason for the mall trip was for Bryston to pick up the shoes that Bethany had fallen in love with. She thought they'd be perfect for Destiny. The only problem was that they were out of stock online. Somehow she had managed to find the same pair at a shoe store in the mall so she sent Bryston and Destiny to pick them up. Problem solved right? Wrong.

"What shoes?" Bryston asked carelessly, his attention now engulfed on his phone.

Bethany snatches him up by the ear.

"Ow Ma! Dang."

Bethany was fuming.

"The shoes that we sent you to get her for our company party tonight."

He silently slides his phone on the end table and snaps, as if it all came back to him.

"Right. Those shoes."

Bradley grew frustrated and seemed to take Bethany's side on the matter as he chimed in.

"Tell me you didn't just buy a bunch of sneakers for yourself, Bryston?"

Now Destiny joined in on the conversation.

"This wouldn't be the first time."

Bryston shoots Destiny a look, mouthing, *I'm gonna kill you.* He hears his dad ask him a question and turns his attention back to him.

"Of course not Dad. You know what? I just realized I forgot a bag at one of the stores. I'm gonna grab it."

"I'm sure," Bradley sarcastically replies.

Bryston swiftly grabs his bags, aiming to get out while he still could.

"And Bryston?" Bethany calls out.

He freezes in his tracks and partially turns to her.

"I suggest that you don't come back into this house without this *bag.*"

"Yes ma'am," was all he could get out before racing out the door.

Henry falls forward, plopping down Alexa's remaining four suitcases on top of her new bed. Taking a deep breath, he adjusts his tux jacket, desperately trying to regain his strength.

"If you need me, I'll be in the downstairs foyer," he said before bowing, leaving Alexa who was getting nicely acquainted with her room.

<<<<<<<<<<<<<<<<<<<<<<<<<<<<<<<<<<<<<<

"But do y'all see this throne chair tho?"

Alexa yelled, holding up her phone in front of her. Serenity, Laila, and Kyrie were on a group Facetime call with her. She walked over to the throne chair and flipped the camera view so that they could get a better view.

"Yo Lex, you got it made up in Bel Air," Kyrie exclaimed.

"You ain't neva lie," Serenity added.

In that moment a major thought hit Alexa harder than ever. Her life that she once knew in Harlem was no more. Still refusing to accept it, she responded.

"Facts but I'mma still be me regardless. Shoot, there's a new Bel Air Princess in town."

# CHAPTER 5

""OH I GET IT, THEY PAINTIN' ME OUT TO BE

THE BAD GUY

WELL IT'S THE LAST TIME YOU'RE GONNA SEE

A BAD GUY DO THE RAP GAME LIKE ME"

-NICKI MINAJ

# I'd Like to Take a Minute Just Sit Right There

Heavy bass rumbles through Alexa's new room. The walls slightly vibrate along with each bass THUMP from the song's beat.

*Hips tick-tock when I dance
On that Demon Time, she
might start an Only Fans
Big B and that B stand for bands
If you wanna see some real ass,
baby, here's your chance*

Alexa twerks along to the music as she rummages through her suitcases. Her hips rotate in a circular motion. She pulls out jeans and tosses them into a pile she concocted on the huge bed.

*I say; left cheek, right cheek, drop it low, then swang*

"Ayeee," she yelled and threw her hand up with her tongue out.

"Texas up in this thang, put you up on this game, IVY PARK on my frame, Gang, gang, gang, gang."

Her task of unpacking was quickly kissed goodbye as club turn up was on and poppin'. In mid push up twerk, the music cut off. Alexa swung her head around, ready to confront whoever interrupted her song. She spots the intruder and her frown is replaced with a genuine smile.

"Don't let me interrupt," the little voice giggled out.
Alexa smirked simultaneously with an eyebrow raise.

"Hi Alexa. I'm your cousin, Destiny."

"Hi cousin Destiny. I'm Alexa."

Alexa was amazed with such maturity coming from such a little girl.

Destiny lets out another one of her contagious giggles and hands Alexa an elegant white couture gown with a pearl set of earrings and matching pearl necklace.
The gown was protected by a clear dress cover.

"Mom told me to give this to you. It's for their company party tonight."

"Party?"

From the confused look on Alexa's face, Destiny took the liberty on filling her in.

"Yes, Mom and Dad's firm just won a major case."

Partially wanting to know, Alexa perked her ears up while she hung up the gown in the walk-in closet.

"Oh really? Spill the tea girl."

"Spill the tea?"

Seeing the "I have no idea what you mean" look on her cousin's face, Alexa simply shook her head. She had finished hanging up the gown and lay on the bed.

"Meaning, give me the scoop."

Destiny's eyes echoed her understanding of this new hip term.

"But isn't that just telling everyone's business?"

"Well yeah, that's the point."

An awkward pause lingered in the room as Destiny desperately tried to put two and two together.

"I don't get it."

Alexa let out an exhausted sigh.

"Never mind. Tell Aunt Beth thanks for me."

Deciding to get back to her task originally at hand, she peeled herself off of the bed, and began tossing around a new batch of clothes from yet another suitcase. Destiny stood by her bed, silently watching her. She's goes into a deep thought and contemplates her next move.

"Hey Alexa?"

"Yeah?"

Alexa tosses clothes over her shoulder keeping her attention on rummaging through her things.

"Can you teach me how to dance?"

Alexa freezes in mid toss. Thinking that she had misheard her, she stays silent for a few moments.

"Alexa?" Destiny repeated, anxiously awaiting her answer.

"Oh you were serious. Got it," Alexa says but suddenly wishes she hadn't.

"Auditions for our school's dance team are on Monday and I'm super nervous."

Destiny joins Alexa on her bed while Alexa hesitates to respond. Everything in her is screaming to not get involved in her cousin's dilemma, but there was something about Destiny that reminded Alexa of her younger self.

<<<<<<<<<<<<<<<<<<<<<<<<<<<<<<<<<<

Maybe it was something about the sadness in her eyes. I remember I had those same eyes at my very first ballet recital. I was the only girl in my class to land a solo and wanted nothing more than to look out to the crowd and see my mom barely contain her excitement as she was to witness her baby's first solo. Deep down I already knew that she wasn't going to be there but I imagined it in my mind. My dad, on the other hand, had taken off work just to see me do my thang. Saying I was all types of nervous is an understatement. My ballet instructor, Miss Saige, taught us to tap into our innermost confidence whenever we stepped on the stage. When we were in doubt, we would mantra it out. She would have us repeat, *I am smart enough, I am brave enough, I am talented enough. I am strong enough and I am an Amazing dancer.* And just like that, I was a girl on fire lightin' up the stage.

Miss Saige was my coach and personal guru. A part of me wanted to be that role model to Destiny. Besides, I couldn't let her go out like that. Now granted, I'm no miracle worker, but how bad can homegirl be right?

<<<<<<<<<<<<<<<<<<<<<<<<<<<<<<<<<

"What if I'm not good enough?"

Destiny asked with pain tied onto each word. It was clear to Alexa that she placed the pressure on herself to be perfect at whatever she did.

"Hey! None of that, aight?"

She slid off the bed, grabbing and dragging Destiny's hand with her.

Gently she says, "Repeat after me. I am amazing," pairing a hair flip with duck lips for the Gods.

"I am amazing," Destiny recites, smiling from ear to ear.

Alexa figured all Destiny needed was someone to tell her that she's good enough to do anything she puts her mind to. She had to let loose and become unafraid of her body. And she had every intention on teaching her how to do so.

"Okay so first things first. A good dancer always brings the class, the sass, and a whole lot of ass."

She continued to instruct, projecting her new coach like voice. Destiny looked back at her not-so-curvy-butt. Alexa responded knowing exactly what Destiny was thinking.

"No worries it'll come."

She grabbed her sound bar remote and hit the PLAY button. K Camp "Lottery" (Renegade) begins to blare from the speakers.

*Cash on me, like I hit the lottery*

"Now. Let's see what I'm working with."

Alexa yells over the music. She motions for Destiny to follow her lead. She shows her an in and out booty pop combo. Destiny catches onto the combo but is mainly popping her back. After a few tries at the combo Alexa initiates a friendly dance battle. Destiny doesn't back down. She hits dem folks on her one time, kicks her leg straight up and holds it. She ends it with a woe that went right on que with beat of the song.

"Okay. I see you," Alexa screams out, hypin' Destiny up.

Although impressed, she shows her out with a slow than fast milly rock that rolls into her tik tok twerk, left cheek, right cheek to the beat and finishes her off with the push-up twerk. The twerk class comes to a close. Alexa grabs the sound bar remote and pauses the music. They fall to the ground breathing heavy. Feeling utterly exhausted they giggle in between their breaths and high five each other. Managing to finally catch her breath, Alexa picks herself back up on her two feet.

"We did dat. That confidence right there is what you need to bring to your audition. You do that and I guarantee you'll make it."

She helped Destiny stand up.

"Yeah. Thank you for everything."

"That was all you girl," Alexa encouraged.

A sudden knock captured both the girls' attention. Bethany shared a smile before entering the bedroom.

"Destiny baby, can you excuse us for a moment?"

Destiny automatically agrees with her mother.

"Yes."

Bethany inspects the room. Her eyebrow rises when her gaze lands on Alexa's concoction of clothes on the floor and bed. She notices the gown tucked away in the bedroom closet so she takes the gown out, and moves some shirts out of the way before laying it on the bed. Irritation immediately flashes across Alexa's face. She shakes it away, and forces herself to be cordial.

"Destiny filled you in on the party tonight I hope?"

"Yup and Congratulations," Alexa dryly answers.

Bethany motions for her to sit with her.

"Thank you. And I apologize for springing all of this at the last minute. With the case and all, we overlooked the dates."

"It's cool."

"Good. This party means so much to both your uncle and I. Now I know formal isn't really your thing but just remember to relax and when in doubt just refer to Caroline. They may even think you're sisters."

Alexa's body stiffens. Familiar anger shoots through every vain.

<<<<<<<<<<<<<<<<<<<<<<<<<<<<<<<<<<<<
Here she go. Once again I'm left feeling like I don't belong with this family. How dare she ask me to pretend to be like Caroline? Caroline of all people at that. See, I knew it. If she thinks for one second that I'm gonna put on this grandma gown, and act like my boogie cousin just because she thinks I'm *ratchet* and don't own anything nice, she got anotha thing comin'.
<<<<<<<<<<<<<<<<<<<<<<<<<<<<<<<<<<

"Anyway, the party is at seven sharp."

She awkwardly rubs Alexa's arm and starts to head out of the room. "Seven CP time?" Alexa calls out.

Bethany stops dead in her tracks and turns around with a confused look.

"Seven sharp got it," she chuckles.

When Bethany is fully out of sight, Alexa holds the sophisticated gown up to her body and gazes into a huge rhinestone bordered standing mirror. She frowns and throws the gown on the floor.

# CHAPTER 6

"I LICK THE GUN, WHEN I'M DONE 'CAUSE I KNOW, THAT REVENGE IS SWEET, SO SWEET"

-RIHANNA

## *I'll Tell You How I Became the New Princess of a Town Called Bel Air*

A classical song rendition, Pachelbel "Cannon in D" plays softly in the background . The very elaborate, elegant celebration event has begun. Servers with sterling silver serving trays, that are adorned with tasty appetizers and finger foods and tall champagne flutes filled with golden champagne move swiftly around to an abundance of guests that now fill the very elegant living room and lavish backyard. Each room is filled with superb black and gold décor. Bradley and Bethany converse with several of the guests. They stop occasionally to hug or wave hello to incoming guests. Bethany carefully examines the living room, clearly absorbing each and every décor detail.  She was feeling like she went a little overboard when her gaze paused on a marble fountain with a baby angel in the middle of it as chocolate poured from its mouth.

"You think the chocolate fountain was too much?" she asks through a plastered smile.

Bradley throatily laughs.

"Is that a trick question?"
She instinctively rolls her eyes.

"Haha...very funny."

"Seriously. We worked so hard for this moment. Everything has to be perfect."

Wanting to remove all doubt from her mind, Bradley scoops her into his arms. He softly speaks to her.

"And it is. Just relax and take it all in."

She smiles and exhales, feeling a little more relaxed. Her shoulders begin to release the tension that was embedded in them. She's finally starting to relax. She sees her best friend, Amber Redding, and a huge smile appears on her face. Already knowing what his wife was thinking, Bradley leads her to Amber and her fiancé, Kyle Weaver, who happens to be his best friend.

"Boy this White family spares no expense when it comes to throwing a shindig," Alexa thought, her eyes roaming the room.

A handsome young server catches her eye. He looks like a younger version of Bryston Tiller. They stare at each other and for a moment Alexa forgets where she is. After almost running into a guest, the young server breaks eye contact and regains his focus. Alexa contemplates if what they both experienced had truly been a moment or did it just feel like one in her head.

Pushing the thought out of her mind, she reminded herself of the present moment.

She was at this very prestigious event, an event where she had to act like someone else, someone whom she despised with a passion. Tonight she would show them that she refuses to act like anyone but herself. If they thought that she didn't belong there than so be it.

She pulled a piece of gum from out of her clutch and popped it in her mouth. It's show time. She strides into the presence of Bradley and Bethany chomping on her gum.

She looked way too grown for her age. A "hoochie mama" is what her dad would say whenever she showed an excessive amount of skin that wasn't appropriate for a teenager. The skintight bodycon dress that hugged her vastly developing body, was far from anything related to a good girl.

As tempted as she was to put on the gown that her Aunt Bethany had given her, she wanted her point to be made. She was tired of this family shaming her for being herself, so much so that they wanted her to become a robot and do and say what Caroline would and that infuriated her.

They thought she was some hood rat from the slums of Harlem who couldn't dare handle a formal event with company friends. I mean, sure, she cursed sometimes and threw a little slang at them but as much as she hated to, she knew how to conduct herself in the presence of boogie folks.

<<<<<<<<<<<<<<<<<<<<<<<<<<<<<<<<<<

You know, for a split second when Aunt Beth came into my room, I thought that maybe this time things would be different. Clearly I was wrong. I'm tired of this family shaming me for being myself. Shoot, so much so that they want me to become a robot and do and say what Caroline does. I'm heated y'all. I promise you that I'm not just some ratchet chick from Harlem. I know how to act around boogie folk, I mean like dem for real pinkies up while they drink type folk. My nana was one of those types of people. She signed me up for my very first debutant ball when I was 8-years-old. And by sign me up, I mean forced me to do it. She literally trained me. I absolutely hated it at first, but my nana had a charm about her that I couldn't resist. By the end of our training I was a princess with exquisite etiquette, and I actually liked it. After that, she kept me in and coached me - all the way up until last year. It was crazy how she could be so tough yet so loving all at the same time.

If it was up to her she would've made debutante my career, but she moved all the way to Ohio after she married my Pop Pop.

And y'all...she loooooooved to see me dance. I made her cry once when I danced to her favorite song "Angel" by Anita Baker. I worked so hard on it. I literally studied her collection of Alvin Ailey performances and concocted my own routine. Not to toot my own horn, but I killed it. Mind you I hadn't been in any type of dance class yet. After seeing me dance she found and paid for all of my jazz and ballet lessons. Even to this day she'll ask me to dance for her. As long as it is not that "twerking mess" as she would say.

I fell in love with dance the moment my nana walked me into the Dance 411 studio. It's my escape into another world.

As strict as my nana is, she instills so much love into me. No matter how much trouble I get into or cray outfits I wear, she still shows me love.

This family keeps judging me and my dad. Why? Because of where we lived and our swag. Look, New Yorkers have everything from deep accents, impeccable swag, fashion, bomb food, you name it, and we got it. Well, except for manners. They need to just accept that will never be in our nature.

Aunt Beth has no idea about any of this. She never bothered to even try to get to know me. And I'm over it. She goin' to learn today.

<<<<<<<<<<<<<<<<<<<<<<<<<<<<<<<

Alexa sashays through the crowd. Guests stare and murmur when she walks past them. Bethany sees her and does a double take. Already seeing the fire in her eyes, Bradley shoves another glass of champagne into her hands.

"Now honey I..."

Bethany silences him with her finger.

"Your mess, you clean it up," she says with every ounce of venom oozing out from her voice.

They watch as Alexa attempts to sneak a glass of champagne from a server.

"And quick," she adds before she storms off into the kitchen.

Bradley treads over to Alexa, failing to hide his frustration.

"I'mma need 'bout two more of these my guy," he hears her call out to one of the servers.

Just as she's about to drink Bradley snatches it out of her hand.

"What in God's name do you think you're doing?"

"Gettin litty."

"Getting what?"

She rolls her eyes.

"Right. In Bel Air terms, I'm having a spectacular time," she adds flair with a valley girl accent.

Bradley signals for the server to confiscate the drink he's been holding onto.

"Is this some type of joke to you?" he asks in utter disbelief.

Another classical ensemble begins to play.

"No but this music is."

Before Bradley could utter another word, she begins to head over to the DJ booth.

"Aye DJ!" she yelled.

"Alexa!"

Before he can fully extinguish Alexa's souped up Harlem swag he noticed a new storm brewing up in the distance. Bethany's parents had just entered the party.

Meanwhile, Bryston was feeling all gassed up as he watched Destiny squirm uncomfortably. He had accidentally gotten the wrong size for the shoes that he was forced to get during his sneaker therapy run.

How was he supposed to remember Destiny's shoe size? So what if he received several texts and calls from his mother reminding him. She even took the time to input the size into his reminder app on his phone. So what? It was supposed to be his day to get his fill of relaxation.

At first he felt kind of bad sitting there watching Destiny squirm over and over again. But then again, he thought about how much she complained the entire mall trip, completely ruining his moment of relaxation, and felt no remorse for her. Besides, why would she wear a pair of shoes that's one... ugly and two... too small on her feet? He smirks and sips his sparkling water.

"Ugh stupid shoes," she whines, shifting uncomfortably.

"What's the matter? New shoes too much to handle?" he asks still smirking.

"Haha very funny. Wait until mom finds out what you did."

"Look, she said to get the shoes, I got the shoes."

"Yeah in the wrong size, genius."
"Simple solution. Go upstairs and change them."

"No way. Mom would freak. And I don't want to ruin this for her."

"Well, case closed," he says before walking away.

She sticks her tongue out at him.

"Case closed," she says mocking him, and folds her arms.

<<<<<<<<<<<<<<<<<<<<<<<<<<<<<<<

Meet the antique snooties - Aunt Bethany's parents, Denise and Nicholos Walters and both are 50 somethin'.

They can't stand my Uncle Bradley, and feel like it's not too late for Aunt Bethany to find someone else, someone who is more qualified, as if being a lawyer is not qualified enough. Son, these wealthy folks be on one.

I haven't met them. They were always on some exotic vacation that Caroline had no problem bragging about. It was usually flaunted the few times that my father had scraped up enough money for us both to come to Bel Air for Thanksgiving or Christmas. Along with the fact that her super cool grandparents were in Dubai or Paree, Caroline would get showered with Christmas gifts from her parents and grandparents. I remember comparing my doll collection to Caroline's. I couldn't relate.

Now, I can say, as strict as my Nana was and still is, she absolutely spoils me and always sends me some type of gift no matter where she is or where I am.

Anyway, back to the snobbies at hand....

<<<<<<<<<<<<<<<<<<<<<<<<<<<<<<<<<<<

Bradley finally spots Bethany in the crowd and heads over to her. Just as he was about to form a word she stops him.

"Oh my God. They're here," she says mortified.

"You invited them?"

"Of course not."

The Walters spot them out in the crowd and wave them down. Bradley and Bethany plaster smiles on their faces and meet them halfway.

"Mom. Dad. What a surprise," she says giggling awkwardly.

"Hello Bevie."

"Of course we couldn't miss your big moment sweetie."

Bradley clears his throat.

"Mr. and Mrs. Walters, it's good to see you both."

"Bradley," they respond dryly. Stiff handshakes and hugs take place.

"So Bradley where is this niece I've heard so much about?" Denise asks.

"Ah Alexa. She's somewhere around here."

Drake's "Tootsie Slide" begins to blare throughout the party.

*I'ma show you how to get it*
*It go, right foot up, left foot*
*slide*
*Left foot up, right foot slide*
*Basically, I'm saying either way,*
*we 'bout to slide, ayy*

"Yassss," Alexa yells, and moves her body to the beat.

"Good lord. Who is she?" Denise asks, staring at Alexa who is now on the dancefloor.

"That's my niece, Alexa."

They continue to watch as Alexa pulls several guests onto the dance-floor. The guests smile and start to dance offbeat.

"Why am I not surprised," Denise mutters. Bradley shoots his gaze to her.

"Excuse me?"

"Mom, why don't I show you the renovations."

Bethany yanks Denise's hand and leads her to the newly renovated kitchen, leaving Bradley and Nicholos to chat.

"So, uh, Nicholos, how's the business?"

"My business and I intend to keep it that way. And that's Mr. Waters to you."

"Right. Um, my apologies, Mr. Waters. Um, so Alexa will be attending Bel Air Academy alongside Caroline," he says, desperately trying to keep his cool.

"Ah my Caroline how is she?"

"Wonderful. There she is by the pool."

His gaze follows Bradley's as they watch Caroline and a group of preppy high school teens laugh out loud about some inside joke.

"I'll go say hello. Good day Bradley."

Nicholos strides off while Bradley pretends to vomit.

CLING, CLING, CLING.

Once the room goes silent, Bethany makes an announcement.

"Dinner will now be served. Please return to your tables."

Servers begin to place plates of food on each of the beautifully decorated tables. Guest make their way to their designated tables.

Alexa plops down on her seat at the massive table. Destiny sits down next to her, smiles and lays her napkin across her lap. Alexa fumbles with her napkin as dinner plates are placed in front of them.

"Girl, what in the he..., I mean, world, is this?" Alexa asks.

"Chicken Paillard," Destiny replies.
"Interesting."

She sticks a finger in the sauce and then pops her finger in her mouth.

"Mmkay. I can work with it," she says in between smacks.

She reaches down into her neon pink mid-sized clutch and pulls out a small bottle that has red liquid in it.

"Is that hot sauce?" Destiny asks in amazement.

Bethany glances over at them, and is immediately filled with embarrassment.

"Mmhmm girl. You want some?"

"No thank you."

"Aight, you don't know what you missin'."

She pours a heaping amount onto her food and licks the last contents from off of her fingers. Several onlookers look disturbed.

Bethany chuggs her champagne.

"Another please," she says, snapping her fingers at the servers.

Every five seconds Destiny fidgets uncomfortably in her seat as Alexa finally asks her for the reason to her restlessness.

"Okay why do you keep squirming around?"

"My shoes. They're too small."

Alexa glances down at her shoes.

"Girl take dem ugly shoes off then."

"I can't."

"Sooooooo you wanna keep the small shoes on?"

Alexa seems disturbed by her decision to remain in pain, wiping her mouth with her napkin and throwing it to the side.

"Yes. Wait, No," Destiny sighs at her own dilemma.

"I'm confused."

"Mom loves these shoes. This is such a big day for her. I just want her to be happy."

Alexa pulls Destiny's fallen chin back up.

"Hey, you are not in charge of anyone else's happiness but your own."

Destiny smiles.

"You always know the perfect things to say."

"Yup and I say let's get you out of these small ass shoes."

They both laugh and head up the stairs.

"You're in luck. I happen to have some shoes that are the same color and look a hundred times better."

Surprisingly they wore the same size. Destiny always had growing feet and Alexa had such small feet for her growing teenage body.

<<<<<<<<<<<<<<<<<<<<<<<<<<<<<<<<<<<

In mid conversation with a guest, Bethany releases an abnormally loud laugh as she spills a splash of champagne from her glass on Bradley.

"Whoops," she says, slurring her words and bursting into more laughter.

"Okay Honey. I think we had enough here."

He motions for the server.

"I need several bottles of water, stat."

Bradley grabs the champagne glass from out of her hand.

"What're you gonna do, huh? Arrest me Mr. Officer?"

She fumbles out her chair and walks off. Guests at the table watch in horror while Bradley tries to play it down.

"Mark. Julia. Thank you for coming."

"Of course, man. It's always a pleasure. Congratulations again," Mark replied.

They shook hands and exchanged hugs. Immediately after, Bradley tracks her down, grabbing Bethany who has found herself another drink.

"Let's get you some water."

Alexa and Destiny head back downstairs and make their way onto the dancefloor. Destiny is relieved and feels free. She trails behind Alexa holding her hand, feeling like she has found her new best friend. They dance like no one's watching, commanding the dance floor. The feeling of freedom filters through the room and the crowd joins them on the dancefloor as everyone lets loose.

Destiny becomes the center of attention when she starts to put those twerk moves she had learned earlier that day to work. Bradley, Bethany, Bryston, and Caroline's jaws drop.

Bradley has had enough. He rushes through the crowd, and yanks the cords out of the socket, cutting off the DJ's equipment in the middle of Destiny's booty pop.

"Alexa Marie Baldwin," he yelled with his voice roaring through the room.

Bradley waits at the door for the last stragglers to leave.

"Alright, you all drive safe now."

He eases the front door shut and deeply exhales.

# CHAPTER 7

"NOW YOU GOTTA SEE ME WILDING, NOW I'M THE ONE THAT'S LYING AND I DON'T FEEL BAD ABOUT IT"

-BEYONCE

# If Anything, I Could Say That
# This Cab Was Rare

CLANK, CLANK! Bethany gathers up dirty dishes and plops them into the sink. She walks over to the kitchen island, gathers more of the dirty champagne flutes, utensils, and throws them into the sink. Meanwhile,

Henry reluctantly dries the clean plates. He's as quiet as a mouse being sure not to run into hurricane Bethany. The more she reflected on how the evening went, the more she took her emotions out on the dishes. She was grateful Bradley had given her the water when he did or else she wouldn't be able to remember anything in the morning, even though, at first, that was kind of the point.

Henry interrupts her thoughts.

"Madam I'll take it from here."

"I got it Henry. You go."

"I insist," he rebutted back.

"Henry, if you don't take your ass up and out of this kitchen..."

Bethany yanks the dry towel from his hand and begins to dry the plates. Henry happens to bump into Alexa and Destiny on the way out.
"Damn girl you held your own out there. I'm proud of you."

They dap up and giggle.

"Proud of her? Are you out of your damn mind?"

Bethany slams both the towel and plate down on the counter, startling the girls.

"Whoa. Chill Aunt Beth."

"Yeah Ma. You trippin'," Destiny says in her newly discovered hip voice. Bethany's eyebrow shoots up as she puts her hand on her hip.

"Excuse Me?"
Feeling the fire that's blazing out from her eyes, Destiny hides behind Alexa.

"Sorry," she spits out.

"Oh you have no idea how sorry you're going to be. Bed. Now."

"Yes ma'am. Goodnight Lex."
Alexa chucks up the deuces. After a moment of silence, she tugs at her hoops and clears her throat.

"So, uh, you need any help?"

"No and if I did I certainly wouldn't ask you."

"Wow! What's that supposed to mean?"

"The nerve of you to waltz in here like..."

"Like what? A ghetto hood rat from Harlem?"

"Well if the shoe fits."
Alexa scoffs.

"Wow. I knew it. That's what you really think of me huh?"

She flops down onto one of the kitchen stools.

"Oh come on Alexa. Look at you. For God's Sake look at what you're wearing. If this is not who you are then show me otherwise."

"Please. You've been judging me from the moment I walked in."

She flips her hair and turns her attention to her phone.

"No one is judging you Alexa. Look at me when I'm talking to you young lady."

Alexa puts the phone down.

"You have been given the opportunity to turn your life around."

"Opportunity? I didn't want this. I can't be some Bel Air Barbie."

"Where you are does not define who you have to be. If that's the case I would have left."

Alexa sucks her teeth.

"You don't even know what I been through."

"Oh honey, I don't have to."

"But..."

"This conversation is over Alexa. Goodnight."

Bethany cuts out of the kitchen while Alexa fiddles with her overextended press-on nails.

# CHAPTER 8

"I'M MOVING ON I'M
PUTTING ON MY, FREE."

-JHENE AIKO

*But I thought 'Nah, forget it' -*
*'Yo, homes to Bel Air'*


Alexa sits kriss kross applesauce on her bed. She glides her fingers over her yearbook photos, giggling at several photos of her and her best friends in Power Ranger costumes, football jerseys and silly miss matched attire. All of which they wore for their school's spirit week.  Her gaze freezes on a photo of her and Aaron beaming smiles at each other at their homecoming dance. Tears start to form then slowly flow from her eyes.  After shutting the book, she picks up her phone and opens her FaceTime App.

She quickly wipes her runny mascara and nose before jumping off the bed and running to the mirror.  Satisfied with how she looks, after a few hair flips of course, she plops back on the bed and hits the green call button.

"Yooo, wudup big head," Aaron says with a huge smile on his face.

"Hey you," she giggles.

"It feels like I ain't seen you in foreva. How's Cali treatin' you?"

She paused, contemplating if she would tell him all that happened.

"It's definitely different, and I'm still getting my feet wet. But I have a feeling everything will be straight."

"I bet. That's wassup tho."

"Yeah. I miss you like crazy A, like my heart hurts, dead ass."

"I miss you, too, Lex. Every day. And I know things are different and stuff but just do you and be you ma. You got this."

She smiled and gazed into his eyes. Not saying a word for few moments. Really taking in the like/love feeling she was feeling in her heart. He knew her so well. Without her having to even say a word, he had already said everything that she needed to hear.

"Lex...Lex? Damn I think you froze."

"Nah I'm here. You right. Preciate ya," she finally said, snapping out of her daze.

"Look Bae, I gotta go but I'll hit you up in the mornin' aight?"

"Aight."

They kiss the camera at the same time before hanging up. Just then she grabs the remote to the sound bar and hits the play button. Soft ballet music spills out into the room. She slides off the bed and gets into first position. With graceful, yet precise arms and legs, she floats out a ballet routine. In the mist of it, she shuts her eyes, getting lost in the melody.

Bethany lurks in the doorway, silently watching in awe.
In that moment, a feeling of love and admiration flows through her. She realizes that she has to accept Alexa for Alexa, through her roughness and all.

Besides, diamonds are made from applying intense pressure, right?

# CHAPTER 9

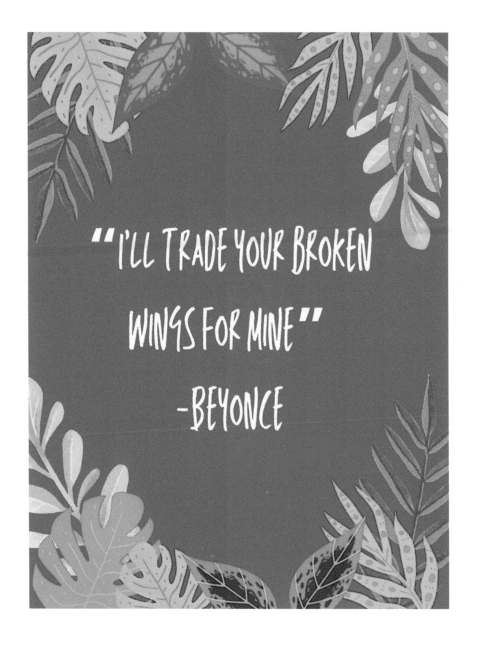

# I Hope They're Prepared For
# The Princess of Bel Air

Okay, so maybe I went a little too far. But my point had to be made. Aunt Beth is right tho. Where I am doesn't have to define who I have to be or change who I already am.

Maybe Bel Air won't be dat bad after all.

<<<<<<<<<<<<<<<<<<<<<<<<<<<<<<<<<
*It's raining men, hallelujah; it's raining men, amen*

Alexa and Destiny sit at the edge of the bed, vibin' to the song.

"Bring dat ass here boy," Alexa yells over the very loud music.

Bryston drags his long legs across the room.

"Ugh. I can't believe you're making me do this."

"Yeah yeah. Payback's a... " Destiny quickly covers Alexa's mouth.

If you enjoyed this book, then I ask you one small favor – would you be kind enough to leave a review for this book on Amazon?

I promise it will be quick and painless.

Thank you for sharing your time and supporting Fresh Princess of Bel Air!

Should you have any questions for me, please feel free to reach out:

MeeksKreations@gmail.com

http://Meekskreations.com

Or visit my social media:
Facebook
@ https://www.facebook.com/tameka.hanley/

Instagram
@ https://www.instagram.com/ms_tamekah29/